MERRITT MEMORIAL SCHOOL

FOR JENNIFER AND GRAHAM

If Mice Could Fly

JOHN CAMERON

Atheneum New York

Copyright © 1979 by John Cameron. Printed in England. All rights reserved. LCCN 79–4927; ISBN 0 689 30731 4

If mice were like monkeys
they'd hang upside down
and bombard the cats
as they strolled on the ground.

And the cats, though hungry
and ready to drop,
would never quite catch
a mouse on the hop.

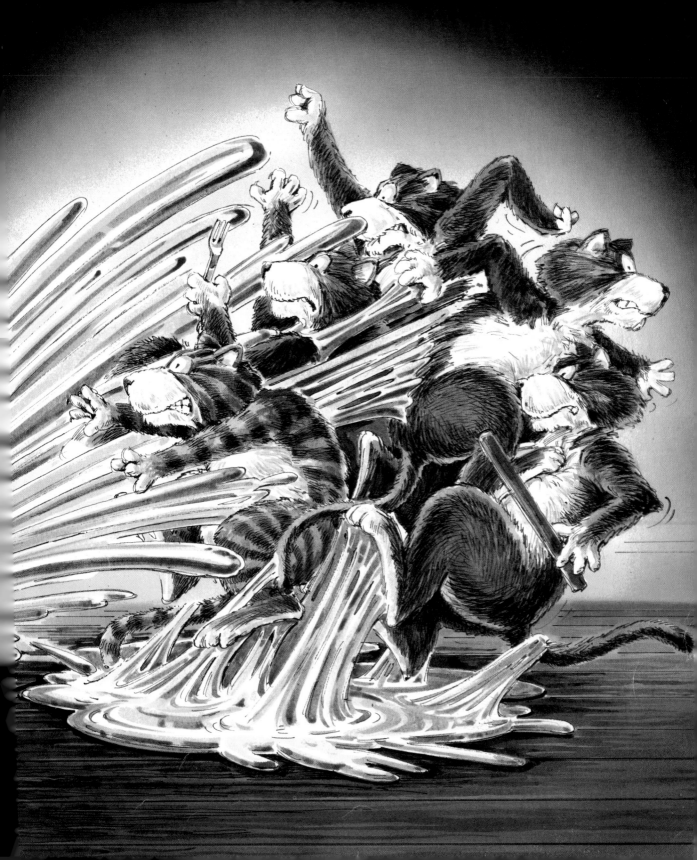

JE
C

#81-06

Cameron, John

If mice could fly

DATE			
OCT 07	FEB 23	OCT 30	
NOV 11		FEB. 07	
JUN 1	OCT 06	JUN. 5	
NOV 18	April	NOV. 7	
NOV 27	KALE		
MAR 17	VerList		
1P	APR 11		
	MAY 8		
NOV 25	MAY 10		
FEB 28	MAY 29		
APR 26			

MERRITT MEMORIAL SCHOOL